Aslan's Triumph

Adapted from
The Chronicles of Narnia
by C. S. Lewis

Illustrated by Deborah Maze

HarperCollins*Publishers*

With special thanks to
Jennifer, Stephanie, Harvest,
Jordan, Becky, and John
—D.M.

A special thanks to Douglas Gresham and the C. S. Lewis Estate
for their invaluable guidance and advice in helping to create
THE WORLD OF NARNIA™ picture books.

Aslan's Triumph. Copyright © 1998 by HarperCollins Publishers, Inc. Text
adapted from *The Lion, the Witch and the Wardrobe*, copyright © 1950 by
C.S. Lewis (Pte) Limited. Copyright renewed 1978 by C.S. Lewis (Pte) Limited.
Illustrations copyright © 1998 by HarperCollins Publishers, Inc.
All rights reserved. Printed in the United States of America.
http://www.harperchildrens.com

Library of Congress Cataloging-in-Publication Data
Aslan's triumph / adapted from The chronicles of Narnia by C. S. Lewis ;
illustrated by Deborah Maze.
    p.   cm.
    Summary: Four children, together with Aslan the lion, finally defeat the
White Witch, and the children become kings and queens of Narnia.
    ISBN 0-06-027638-X. — ISBN 0-06-443575-X (pbk.)
    [1. Fantasy.] I. Maze, Deborah, ill. II. Lewis, C. S. (Clive Staples),
1898–1963. Chronicles of Narnia.
PZ7.A83745 1998   97-28642
[Fic]—dc21   CIP
                                         AC

Typography by Steve Scott

ONE SUMMER, four children whose names were Peter, Susan, Edmund, and Lucy were sent far into the country to stay at the house of Professor Kirke. The very first morning, Lucy stepped through a magical wardrobe into the mysterious land of Narnia. There she had tea with Mr. Tumnus the Faun, who told Lucy all about the wicked White Witch and the spell she had cast over Narnia to make it always winter and never Christmas. Edmund was the next to go through the wardrobe. He met the White Witch, who fed him enchanted Turkish Delight and promised to make him King of Narnia someday—if he brought his brother and sisters to her.

Then one day, all four children stepped through the wardrobe into Narnia. They were befriended by Mr. and Mrs. Beaver, who explained to them that Aslan, the Great Lion, had returned to Narnia and wanted to meet them at the Stone Table. Mr. Beaver told them the old saying that when Aslan returned and two Sons of Adam and two Daughters of Eve sat in the four thrones at Cair Paravel, the great castle by the sea, then it would be the end not only of the White Witch's reign but of her life. Peter, Susan, and Lucy were excited about meeting Aslan. Edmund, however, was still under the spell of the Turkish Delight, and he slipped away to the White Witch's house and betrayed them all. The Witch, furious that Edmund had not brought his brother and sisters to her, made him her prisoner and set off with him to find the children and kill them.

But the Witch's power was already weakening. First, Father Christmas arrived in Narnia, and then spring came, ending the Witch's winter once and for all. The three children and the Beavers reached Aslan and the Stone Table safely. They told Aslan about Edmund, and Aslan sent his army to rescue Edmund from the Witch. When Edmund was brought to the Stone Table, he had a long talk with Aslan that he never forgot. But the Witch was not finished with Edmund yet. . . .

As Edmund was apologizing to the others for having betrayed them, the White Witch herself walked out to the top of the hill and stood before Aslan.

"You have a traitor there, Aslan," she said, pointing at Edmund. "Have you forgotten the Deep Magic that the Emperor put into Narnia at the very beginning? This magic, written on the Stone Table itself, says that every traitor belongs to me as my lawful prey. And so that human creature is mine, and unless I have him all Narnia shall perish."

"I do not deny it," said Aslan. And he and the Witch began talking together in low voices.

"The Witch has renounced the claim on your brother's blood," said Aslan at last. After the Witch had left, Aslan told them they had to leave the Stone Table and camp that night at the Fords of Beruna. During the first part of the journey, Aslan advised Peter on the best ways to fight the battle against the Witch. For the last part of the journey, Aslan seemed sad, and Lucy and Susan felt sure something dreadful was going to happen to him. That night, they crept out of their tent to look for him and found him walking into the wood. His tail and his head hung low, and he walked slowly as if he were very, very tired. They followed him up the steep slope toward the Stone Table.

"Oh, children, why are you following me?" Aslan said suddenly, turning around.

"Please, may we come with you—wherever you're going?" asked Susan.

"Yes, you may come," Aslan said after some thought, "if you will promise to stop when I tell you and leave me to go on alone."

They promised, and forward they went again, one girl on each side of the Lion. When they were almost at the top, Aslan said, "Children, here you must stop. And whatever happens, do not let yourselves be seen. Farewell." Both girls cried and kissed him good-bye.

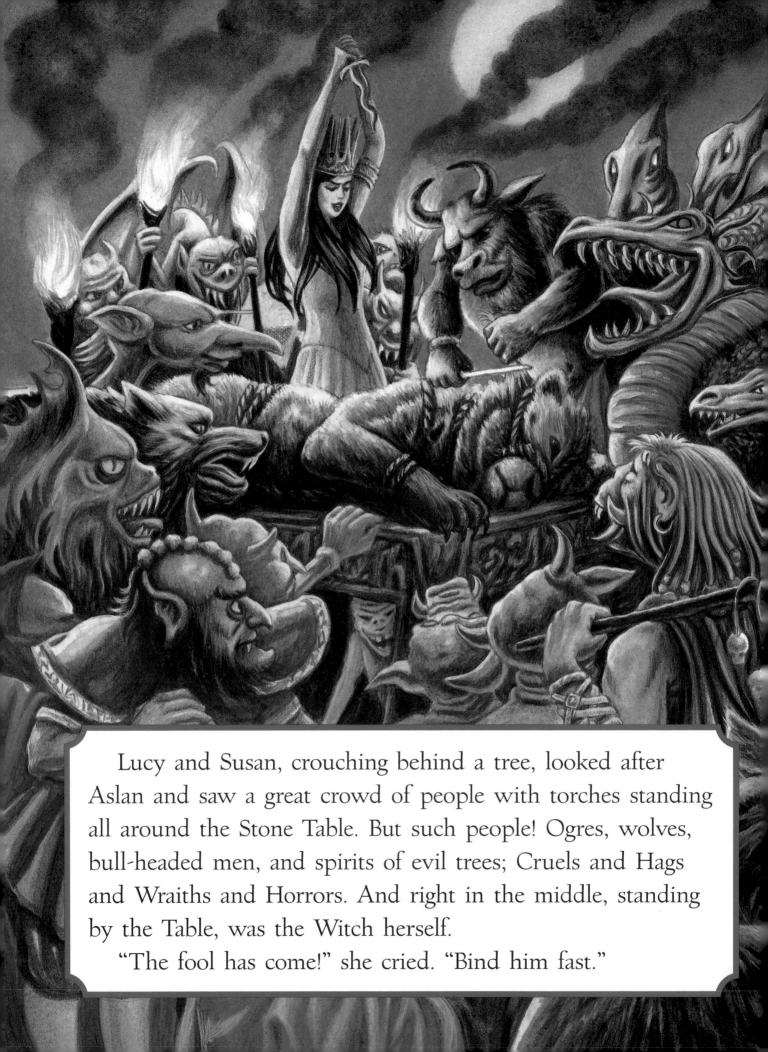

Lucy and Susan, crouching behind a tree, looked after Aslan and saw a great crowd of people with torches standing all around the Stone Table. But such people! Ogres, wolves, bull-headed men, and spirits of evil trees; Cruels and Hags and Wraiths and Horrors. And right in the middle, standing by the Table, was the Witch herself.

"The fool has come!" she cried. "Bind him fast."

Aslan did not resist or make any noise, even when the whole crowd of creatures jeered at him and shaved him, muzzled him, beat him, and tied him tightly with ropes. Then the Witch began to whet her knife.

The children did not see the actual moment of the killing. They couldn't bear to look and covered their eyes. Then they heard the Witch cry, "Follow me! It will not take us long to crush them now that the great Fool, the great Cat, lies dead." With wild cries, the terrible crowd swept down the hill right past where Susan and Lucy were hiding.

As soon as the wood was silent again, Susan and Lucy crept out. They knelt in the grass beside Aslan and kissed his cold face and cried till they could cry no more. Then they unbound the muzzle. They tried to untie the cords, but the knots were too tight.

Hours seemed to go by, and the two girls hardly noticed that they were getting colder and colder. But at last, Lucy saw that the sky was a little less dark than it had been.

And then she noticed some little gray mice moving about on Aslan's body. Susan raised her hand to frighten them away, but Lucy said, "Wait!" They watched in fascination as the mice nibbled away at Aslan's cords until one by one the ropes were all gnawed through. Aslan looked more like himself without them.

As dawn approached, Lucy and Susan walked to the eastern edge of the hill and looked out toward the sea and Cair Paravel. At that moment, they heard from behind them a great cracking, deafening noise.

The two girls ran back to the Stone Table. It was broken into two pieces by a great crack that ran from end to end; and there was no Aslan.

"Is it magic?" cried Susan. "Is it more magic?"

"Yes!" said a great voice behind them. "It is more magic." They looked around. There, shining in the sunrise, stood Aslan himself.

"Aren't you dead then, dear Aslan?" said Lucy.

"Do I look it?" he said.

"But what does it all mean?" asked Susan finally, after both girls had covered him with kisses.

"It means," said Aslan, "that though the Witch knew the Deep Magic, there is a magic deeper still that she did not know. If she had looked further back to before the dawn of Time, she would have known that when a willing victim who had committed no treachery was killed in a traitor's stead, the Table would crack and Death itself would start working backward. And now, children, I feel my strength coming back to me. Oh, children, catch me if you can!" He made a leap high over their heads, and a mad chase began.

"And now," said Aslan presently, "I am going to roar. Put your fingers in your ears."

When Aslan opened his mouth to roar, his face became so terrible that they did not dare to look at it. They saw all the trees in front of him bend before the blast of his great roaring. Then the children climbed onto his warm, golden back, and he shot off, faster than any horse could go, down the hill and into the thick of the forest, across sunny glades and heathery mountains and through wild orchards. That ride was perhaps the most wonderful thing that ever happened to them in Narnia.

It was nearly midday when they found themselves looking down a steep hillside at a castle. Aslan rushed down and jumped right over the castle wall. The two girls tumbled off his back and found themselves in the middle of a wide stone courtyard full of statues. Immediately, Aslan bounded up to a stone lion and breathed on him. Then he pounced on a tall dryad and turned quickly aside to breathe on a stone rabbit and two centaurs. Suddenly, everywhere the statues were coming to life. The courtyard was now a blaze of colors, and the whole place rang with the sound of happy roarings, brayings, yelpings, barkings, cooings, shouts, and laughter. But the best of all was when Lucy found Mr. Tumnus, and Aslan breathed on him. A moment later, Lucy and the little Faun were holding hands and dancing around and around for joy.

After Aslan had brought all the statues to life, he cried, "If the Witch is to be finally defeated, we must find the battle at once."

So they set off in search of the battle. Soon Lucy heard shouts and the clashing of metal against metal. Then she saw Peter and Edmund and all the rest of Aslan's creatures fighting desperately against the Witch's army, and Peter was fighting against the Witch. Aslan gave a great roar that shook all Narnia from the western lamp-post to the eastern sea and flung himself upon the Witch. Peter's tired army cheered, the newcomers roared, and the battle was all over in a few minutes.

The next thing Lucy knew, Peter and Aslan were shaking hands. Peter told Aslan, "It was Edmund's doing. The Witch was turning our troops into stone right and left, but he had the sense to smash the Witch's wand, which gave us a chance. He was terribly wounded."

They went to Edmund, and Lucy poured a few drops of the precious cordial, a gift that had been given to her by Father Christmas, into her brother's mouth. Lucy wanted to stay with Edmund, but Aslan reminded her that there were other wounded, and for the next half hour, she attended to them while he restored those who had been turned to stone. When Lucy returned to Edmund, he was not only healed of his wounds but looked better than he had for a long time. He had become his real old self again, and there on the field of battle Aslan made him a knight.

The next day, everyone began the march eastward to the castle of Cair Paravel. They reached the castle on the following day. Aslan solemnly crowned the four children in the Great Hall. "Once a king or queen in Narnia, always a king or queen. Bear it well, Sons of Adam! Bear it well, Daughters of Eve!" he said.

That night, there was a great feast and revelry and dancing. But amid all these rejoicings, Aslan himself quietly slipped away.

For, as Mr. Beaver explained, "He'll be coming and going. He'll often drop in. Only you mustn't press him. He's not a *tame* Lion, you know."

These two Kings and two Queens governed Narnia well, and long and happy was their reign. Peter became a great warrior and was called King Peter the Magnificent. Susan grew into a tall and gracious woman with black hair that fell

almost to her feet and was called Susan the Gentle. Edmund was a grave and quiet man and was called King Edmund the Just. As for Lucy, she was always gay and golden-haired and was called Lucy the Valiant.

One year, these two Kings and two Queens were hunting the White Stag in the Western Woods when they came upon a tree of iron with a lantern set on the top. As they drew nearer, they all remembered that the thing was called a lamp-post, and then they noticed that they were making their way not through branches but through coats. The next moment, they came tumbling out of a wardrobe into the empty room, and they were no longer Kings and Queens but just four children in their old clothes. It was the same day and hour in which they had first stepped into the wardrobe.

And that is the very end of the adventure of the wardrobe, but it was only the beginning of the adventures of Narnia.

The Great
Waterfall

The
Lamppost

THE LANTERN WASTE

Mr.
Tumnus's
Cave

The
White Witch's
House

ETTINSMOOR

RIVER

SHRIBBLE

Beavers
Dam

THE

GREAT

RIVER

The
Stone Table

RUSH

RIVER

Cair
Paravel

Dancing
Lawn

Glasswater

A MAP OF NARNIA